The Three Little Pigs

Three little pigs
went out into the world.

The first little pig met
a man carrying straw.

The little pig asked,
"May I have some straw
so I can build a house?"

"Yes," said the man.
"You can have some straw."

The first little pig
took the straw.
He built a straw house.

A wolf came along and
knocked on the door.
"Little pig, little pig,
let me come in."

"Not by the hair
of my chinny, chin, chin!"
said the little pig.

"Then I'll huff,
and I'll puff,
and I'll blow your house in,"
said the wolf.

And he huffed.
And he puffed.
And he blew the house in.
And he ate up the first little pig.

The second little pig
met a man carrying sticks.

The little pig asked,
"May I have some sticks
so I can build a house?"

“Yes,” said the man.
“You can have some sticks.”

The second little pig
took the sticks.

He built
a stick house.

A wolf came along and
knocked on the door.
"Little pig, little pig,
let me come in."

"Not by the hair
of my chinny, chin, chin!"
said the little pig.

"Then I'll huff,
and I'll puff,
and I'll blow your house in,"
said the wolf.

And he huffed.
And he puffed.
And he blew the house in.

And he ate up the second little pig.

The third little pig met
a man carrying bricks.

The little pig asked,
"May I have some bricks
so I can build a house?"

"Yes," said the man.
"You can have some bricks."

The third little pig
took the bricks.

He built a brick house.

A wolf came along and
knocked on the door.
“Little pig, little pig,
let me come in.”

"Not by the hair
of my chinny, chin, chin!"
said the little pig.

"Then I'll huff,
and I'll puff,
and I'll blow your house in,"
said the wolf.

And he huffed, and he puffed.
And he huffed, and he puffed.
He could not blow the brick house in.

The wolf was angry.
He jumped on the roof.
He yelled, "Little pig,
I'm coming down the chimney.
I'm going to eat you up!"

But the little pig was smart.
He was smarter than the wolf.
He had a big pot of hot water
in the fireplace.

The little pig lifted the cover.
The wolf fell into the pot.

The little pig lived happily
in his little brick house.